CHOOSE-YOUR-FATE   ADVENTURE BOOK

Super-Villains Strike

BATMAN created by Bob Kane

STARSCAPE

This is a work of fiction. All of the characters, organizations, and events portrayed in this novel are either products of the author's imagination or are used fictitiously.

BATMAN: SUPER-VILLAINS STRIKE:
CHOOSE-YOUR-FATE ADVENTURE BOOK

Copyright © 2012 DC Comics.

Batman and all related characters and elements are trademarks of and © DC Comics. [s12]

CMA25255

A Starscape Book
Published by Tom Doherty Associates, LLC
175 Fifth Avenue
New York, NY 10010

www.tor-forge.com

ISBN 978-0-7653-6481-4

First Edition: May 2012

Printed in the United States of America by
Offset Paperback Manufacturers, Dallas, Pennsylvania.

0 9 8 7 6 5 4 3 2 1

How to Read This Book

You are Batman. You control your own destiny in the story you are about to read. How? At the end of each chapter, you will be asked to make a choice about what you do next. In some chapters, you will be asked to solve a puzzle that will provide a clue to help you make your choice. Occasionally you will come to a chapter that closes with "THE END." When that happens, you can go back to the beginning of the book and start again, making different choices, resulting in different outcomes.

Remember, whatever happens in the story happens because of the choices you make. So choose wisely, and get ready for the adventure of a lifetime ... or *two* ... or *ten* ... or *twenty*!

1

YOU are Batman.

You move like a shadow through the Gotham City night. Arriving at the base of a high-rise glass and steel building, pausing to make sure you remain unseen, you fire a Batrope up into the inky darkness. Tugging on the thin but sturdy line to make sure it's taut, you begin your journey upward.

You climb up the side of the tall apartment building, step by step, hand over hand, pulling yourself up by the Batrope. You are responding to the latest in a series of cat burglaries of luxury, high-rise apartments.

In every one of these recent robberies, there was no sign of forced entry through the door, you think to yourself, running over the details of the cases again and again in your mind. *And only very small but extremely valuable pieces of jewelry were taken.*

No matter how many times you examine the details, you can come to only one conclusion.

Catwoman! you think. *All the crimes bear the earmarks of Catwoman.*

Simple enough, right? Except for one thing. Catwoman is safely behind bars at Arkham Asylum, the maximum security facility for the criminally insane. You know this because you put her there yourself.

So up you climb, slicing through the blackness, silently, stealthily, glancing left, then right, searching both for clues and for any sign of an intruder. Reaching the window of the latest burglarized apartment, thirty stories above the busy Gotham pavement, you pause.

Like the windows of the other burglarized apartments, this window too has tiny scratch marks near the locks, marks that would be invisible to all but the most trained eyes—your eyes, the eyes of Batman!

Once again—Catwoman. I'm sure of it!
Suddenly you hear a noise from above.

What should you do?

If you think you should climb up to investigate the noise, go to Chapter 22.

If you think you should slip around the corner of the building to hide, go to Chapter 39.

2

You spot Mr. Freeze. He scampers up to the top of a water slide, sending startled park visitors scrambling. You fling a Batrope around a tree branch next to the slide and swing up to the top to reach him.

But Mr. Freeze quickly fires his Freeze Gun at the rushing water, freezing the water slide into an icy slope. Then he takes a seat, slides down the frozen ramp, and takes off again, running at top speed.

You drop back to the ground and give chase. Freeze heads into the mouth of a giant clown ride. Reaching the ride, you vault over the top and land at the back end, ahead of Freeze. As he exits, you fling a Batarang at him that knocks the Freeze Gun from his hands.

"Game over, Freeze!" you announce defiantly. "You're going to tell me exactly how you and the others got out of Arkham."

"I'm afraid all I can give you is the cold shoulder!" Freeze cracks back.

Pulling out a tiny remote control device, Mr. Freeze uses it to operate his Freeze Gun, which is lying on the ground. The weapon fires, sending out powerful freezing beams in several directions. You manage to twist out of the way of most of the blasts, but one of the beams catches you on the left shoulder. You grab the frozen, stinging spot with your right hand.

If you think you should go right to Arkham Asylum, go to Chapter 16.

If you think you should fire a grapnel line and swing away, go to Chapter 57.

3

"I think we should try to dig a bit deeper, Doctor," you suggest.

"Certainly, Batman," Dr. Arkham agrees. "Let me get my records for you."

You flip through the logs, trying to find more clues, something—anything—to give you a clearer picture of what is going on.

Your mind keeps going back to the power surge that followed the power outage; you feel that somehow the answer to all your questions is right in front of you. Maybe something else in the records will help you focus on the truth.

Suddenly, you get another message about Catwoman and the Cat's-Eye Diamond. You feel compelled to catch her, despite the fact that you just saw her sitting in her cell here at Arkham. You battle back and forth in your own mind about what to do.

If you think you should go after Catwoman, go to Chapter 29.

If you think you should stay at Arkham, go to Chapter 54.

4

You race to the museum. This all began with Catwoman. Maybe the answer lies with her. Screeching to a stop, you leap from the Batmobile, filled with a new sense of determination. It's one thing to battle your most dangerous enemies. It's quite another to be taken for a ride by copycats pretending to be the criminals.

Inside the museum, you find Catwoman lifting herself up toward the high, painted ceiling of the museum's Gem Room. You see the precise, laser-cut hole in the glass display case from which Catwoman has extracted the Cat's-Eye Diamond.

"Too late, Batman!" Catwoman purrs, the satisfaction obvious in her voice. "This cat has just gotten her third eye."

You realize that she's headed for the roof. Dashing out into the hall, you spy an open window.

Got to beat her to the roof, you think. *Faster if I do it on the outside.*

You climb out the window and begin scrambling up the side of the museum. Like a mountain climber, you use window ledges and ornamentation attached to the building as hand and foot holds to shimmy your way to the roof.

Climbing up and over a huge stone carving of a gargoyle, you drop onto the roof just as Catwoman emerges from a skylight.

"Who are you?" you demand. "I know you're not the real Catwoman. I just saw her in Arkham."

"Why, Batman, I'm hurt that you don't recognize me," Catwoman coos. "We've known each other for such a long time, too. Of course it's me, silly boy. Could a faker do this?"

Catwoman does a handstand on the edge of the roof, then drops off the other side. As you race across the roof to see what trick she has set up, the receiver on your Utility Belt begins to beep.

You receive a report that a small explosion has occurred at the power plant at that exact moment.

There goes the copycat theory, you think. Or at least a single copycat. Obviously someone is pretending to be Poison Ivy at the same time as I'm dealing with this fake Catwoman here. No one can be in two places at once.

If you think you should stay and continue battling Catwoman, go to Chapter 35.

If you think you should leave the museum and go to the power plant, go to Chapter 15.

5

You realize that Poison Ivy is not likely to detonate the explosives all around the power plant while she is still there. You take the gamble and climb up the electric tower.

Seeing this, Poison Ivy scrambles down the opposite side of the tower. You anticipate the path of her descent and, swinging like an Olympic gymnast on the high bars, you fly across the center of the tower, landing on the opposite side.

You swiftly don your breathing mask to avoid Poison Ivy's spell, and you reach for the detonator. She pushes back hard, and the two of you fall from the tower, fifty feet above the cement slab at its base.

Putting one arm around Poison Ivy's waist, you fire a grapnel line up with the other. It catches a crossbeam on the tower. Holding tight both to the line and to your prey, you jerk to a stop, mere inches from the slab.

As Poison Ivy struggles to get free from your grasp, you reach out and snatch the detonator from her hand. At that same moment, Poison Ivy sprays a cloud of pheromones right in your face.

Although your mask protects you from its chemical intoxicant, the gas creates a momentary smoke screen, allowing Poison Ivy to slip from your grasp and get away.

If you think you should try to follow Poison Ivy, go to Chapter 49.

If you think you should go to the reservoir to stop Mr. Freeze, go to Chapter 33.

6

Before checking the sewers of Gotham, you decide to search some of the Joker's other lairs. You arrive at an old factory that you know had been one of the Joker's hideouts off and on for years.

Suddenly you hear something moving in the darkness. Shining a light in the direction of the sound, you spot a huge vining plant. Reacting to the light, the plant shoots several vines in your direction. You roll out of the way and hurry from the factory. But you realize that Poison Ivy has been here. You're on the right track.

You travel next to an abandoned storage ware-house, filled with old furniture. Exploring the stacks of chairs and couches and tables, you come upon one section of the room in which all the furniture is completely encased in ice.

Again, an obvious clue that one of the four escapees has been here.

As you leave the factory, you see a piece of fabric nailed to the back of the door. Unlike everything else in this factory, the fabric seems new.

I remember that the Joker once had a hideout in an old textile mill near the waterfront. This could be a clue trying to send me there. But it reeks of a trap.

If you think you should go to the textile factory, go to Chapter 18.

If you think you should follow your original hunch and check the sewers, go to Chapter 44.

7

You get the feeling that all this running and chasing is just that—a pointless wild goose chase. Mr. Freeze seems to be leading you on a crazy ride through the frozen water park rather than confronting you directly, as he has always done in the past.

Once again, you can't help but think that this chase is simply a distraction and that your time would be better spent back at the Batcave. Every time you

go there, however, something else seems to happen, as if all these escaped criminals are trying to keep you on the move, to keep you guessing.

Still, following Mr. Freeze around a water park, dodging blasts from his Freeze Gun, is not getting you anywhere.

Best to head back to the Batcave and try to make sense of all this.

THIZZZZ!

Suddenly, a blast from Mr. Freeze's Freeze Gun streaks past your ear. He's on the attack again!

If you think you should chase after Mr. Freeze and try to stop him now, go to Chapter 13.

If you think you should leave the water park, go to Chapter 57.

8

You are puzzled by the Riddler's riddle. It seems like just a foolish insult. As with so many aspects of this case, you believe that the Riddler is just trying to distract you, to sidetrack you, to send you on yet another pointless errand.

You decide to ignore the riddle for now and focus on catching Catwoman. Returning to the museum, you spot her tracks— after all these years of battling Catwoman, you are by now quite familiar with the distinctive pattern left by the tread on the bottom of her boots.

Following her trail, you wind your way through the city streets.

Eventually, she leads you to the edge of the city and right to an abandoned factory. You can even see which window she has used to get inside. It remains open.

If you think you should follow Catwoman into the factory, go to Chapter 29.

If you think you should go to Arkham to try to figure out the Riddler's clue, go to Chapter 48.

9

You decide to rush off to the Gotham Water Park. Speeding to the park in the Batmobile, you screech to a stop at the front entrance. As you race through the main gate, an astounding sight greets your eyes. There, in the middle of summer, stands a security guard completely encased in ice.

You dash into the park, not quite sure how to help the guard. Once inside, you encounter a crowd of upset people, all in their bathing suits, pointing at the giant water slide.

A quick glance at it reveals what everyone is so upset about. All the water on the tall slide is frozen solid.

"How did this happen?" you ask the crowd.

"Some weird guy in a moon suit carrying a crazy-looking high-tech rifle shot the water slide and it froze solid!" one person explains.

"Are we going to get a refund for the admission price?" another asks.

This sounds like the work of Mr. Freeze! you think. *But like Catwoman and Poison Ivy, Mr. Freeze is supposed to be locked up in Arkham Asylum.*

If you think you should go back to the Batcave, go to Chapter 58.

If you think you should do a chemical analysis on the frozen water, go to Chapter 46.

If you think you should continue to investigate at the water park, go to Chapter 2.

10

You charge at Mr. Freeze. As he fires again, you dive flat out and land belly first on the ice. You glide along the frozen surface atop the reservoir as Mr. Freeze's latest blast rips past you, just above your back.

You spring back up and snatch the Freeze Gun from his hands. Swinging the butt of the gun, you slam it into Freeze, knocking him to the ice. Then you rip the power pack from the base of the gun, rendering it inoperative.

"Now, Freeze, we are going to have a little talk," you snarl. "About Arkham and your fellow criminals and everything that's been going on!"

Suddenly a noise catches your attention. You recognize the unmistakable sound of stone cracking. You realize that the pressure of all this ice against its walls is starting to create fractures in the dam.

You pull a contraption from your Utility Belt. You created this device in the Batcave using the chemical analysis from the frozen water sample you took earlier. Anticipating a follow-up battle with Mr. Freeze, you brought it with you.

Hurrying to the top of the dam, you flip on the device, which emits a sonic frequency. The sound waves reverse the effects of Mr. Freeze's Freeze Gun. The ice begins to melt, returning the water in the reservoir to normal and relieving the pressure on the dam.

But during the process Mr. Freeze slips away. You still need answers and you wonder whether or not you should chase after Mr. Freeze to try to learn the truth about what's been going on with all these Arkham escapees.

HIDDEN MESSAGE

Find the hidden message in the following sentence:

If you think you should chase after Mr. Freeze, go to Chapter 33.

If you think you should go stop Poison Ivy from blowing up the power plant, go to Chapter 5.

11

Time for riddles later! you think. *I've got the Riddler here in my sight and I'm not letting him get away.*

You speed after the getaway chopper, pushing your Bat-Copter's engine to the limit.

Suddenly a thick steel net fires out from the back of the chopper. It entangles the Bat-Copter's blades and ensnares you in its impenetrable mesh. You are trapped and you can't break free. With its blade stopped, the Bat-Copter tumbles to the ground.

THE END

12

No, you think. This is too convenient. Follow Catwoman into a dark alley? This smells like a trap. I'll just have to pick up the chase another time.

Slipping back into the dark Gotham night, you make your way to the Batmobile. Racing through the streets, you return to the Batcave, where you enter the night's events into the main database of the Batcomputer.

The next morning, as Bruce Wayne, in your office at the headquarters of Wayne Enterprises, you sort through e-mails as you ponder the previous night's events. Your phone rings. The ID tells you that the caller is Lucius Fox, your right-hand man and a pillar of Wayne Enterprises.

"Good morning, Lucius," you say, punching the speakerphone button. "What's up?"

"Got a few minutes, Bruce?" Lucius asks.

"For you, Lucius? Always," you reply. "I'll be right over."

Glad for the break from the avalanche of e-mails that greets you each morning, you hurry down the hall to Lucius Fox's office. Stepping in, you see that Lucius is intently staring at his computer monitor.

"Take a look at this, Bruce," Lucius says.

You scoot around behind his desk as Lucius points to the monitor.

"This new company is looking for investors," Lucius explains. "It looks intriguing to me. They are developing a new communications device that they claim will revolutionize video games. They say that they have developed a breakthrough technology that will produce the most realistic images ever seen."

"Hmm," you say. "It does sound interesting. But this is odd—there's practically no information about the parent company. That makes me a bit uneasy. Still, if they can really do what they say they can do here, this could be a significant investment for us and—"

You are interrupted by the sudden beeping of a news monitor. It runs twenty-four hours a day in your office and in Lucius' office so you can stay in touch with breaking news.

"There's been an explosion at the Gotham Chemical factory," the voice on the newsfeed says.

If you think you should stay at Wayne Enterprises and continue to research the communications company, go to Chapter 36.

If you think you should change into Batman and investigate the explosion in the chemical factory, go to Chapter 30.

13

You take off after Mr. Freeze. As you chase him through the water park, he turns back and fires a wall of ice from his Freeze Gun. You skid to a slippery stop and narrowly avoid crashing into the wall.

Racing around the wall of ice, you catch a glimpse of Mr. Freeze climbing up an artificial mountain. You can see a waterfall rushing off the top of the mountain.

Reaching the base of the mountain, you fire a grapnel line and begin climbing up. Suddenly Mr. Freeze appears, whipping his Freeze Gun around an outcropping and firing icy blasts right at you.

Using all your mountaineering skill and agility, you swing out, away from the mountain, as the first blast rips past you, mere inches from your head. Mr. Freeze fires again, and you swing free of the blast, which shatters into a million tiny icicles on the ground below.

Up you climb, hands moving swiftly, one over the other, your feet bouncing from ledge to ledge. Finally you reach the top. There you spot Mr. Freeze firing his Freeze Gun right into the water as it cascades over the lip of the mountain and runs down the other side.

The waterfall comes to a sudden stop, as if someone has hit a "pause" button. Freeze smiles at you, then fires another blast in your direction. You squat, allowing the blast to pass harmlessly overhead.

That's when Freeze leaps off the mountain and slides down the frozen waterfall at breakneck speed.

You dash across the top of the mountain, take a deep breath, then jump off.

Struggling to keep your feet, you fly down the frozen waterfall like a snowboarder on a snowy hill—only you have no snowboard and you're riding ice, not snow. The soles of your boots skim the surface as the wind pulls hard at your face.

You slide off the bottom of the falls and tumble to a stop. Leaping to your feet, you scan the park in all directions, but can see no sign of Mr. Freeze. He's given you the slip—literally.

If you think you should try to find Mr. Freeze, go to Chapter 2.

If you think you should leave the water park, go to Chapter 57.

14

Caught off guard! you think. *Got to escape before she hits me with her toxins and I lose all these criminals. I'll have to deal with Poison Ivy another time. Catwoman is still leaving clues all over town. Better to go after her.*

You narrowly escape, holding your breath, as Poison Ivy releases a massive blast of toxins. You head off to find Catwoman.

Catwoman's targets seem to be getting smaller— family-owned jewelry stores, tiny art galleries—yet she seems to be purposely taunting you, leaving clues that point directly to her as the perpetrator.

At one location she left a stuffed animal in the shape of a cat that meowed when it was touched. At another she left fake cat whiskers dangling from the front door handle.

Why does she want me to find her? you wonder as you race to the scene of the latest burglary. *Or is it just that she wants me to know that she somehow, despite all the odds, against all logic, has escaped from Arkham?*

Arriving at a display of fabulous jewels in the center of the Gotham City tourist district, you immediately spot the crowd looking and pointing. A police line holds them back and several officers struggle to control the growing mob of curious onlookers.

"What's going on, Officer?" you ask one of the policemen working to hold back the crowd.

"Batman, she appeared out of nowhere," the officer explains, still keeping his attention focused on the crowd. "She jumped from one display cabinet to the next. Before anyone knew what was happening, she had that one open and she emptied it into a sack." The officer pointed up to an empty display case. Its door hung open.

"And what are all these people gawking at," you ask, unable to disguise the annoyance in your voice. Did these people think that witnessing a crime was on the official tour of Gotham City?

"That!" the officer exclaims, pointing to the top of a nearby building.

To your amazement, you look up and see Catwoman perched on a ledge near the top floor of the building. In her black-gloved hand she clutches a large sack. On the sack is a sign that reads: "FOR MY DEAR FRIEND, BATMAN...WITH LOVE, CATWOMAN."

"Taunting" is exactly the word for what she's doing.

But as you pull out a Batrope to give chase, the communicator on your Utility Belt starts beeping. Glancing at it, you are stunned to learn of a bizarre attack at the Gotham Water Park.

If you think you should stay and go after Catwoman, go to Chapter 19.

If you think you should go to investigate the water park, go to Chapter 9.

15

You rush to the power plant. There you find Poison Ivy—or at least whoever is pretending to be Poison Ivy. She has fully rigged the place with explosives. If she sets them off, the resulting blast would be enormous and devastating.

Got to get the detonator away from her or this whole place will blow.

Poison Ivy stands atop a tall metal tower. Electric transformers buzz all around her. She has not yet noticed that you are there.

You realize that if you try to climb up the tower, she would be able to either escape or simply press the detonator button and blow the whole plant sky high.

You snatch a Batarang and take aim at the detonation device that she clutches tightly in her hand. Once you separate her from the device, you'll be able to go directly after her.

You fling the Batarang with a short, sharp flick of your powerful wrist. It cuts through the air on a collision course with Poison Ivy's left hand—the one that grips the detonator.

BEEP!-BEEP!-BEEP!

The receiver on your Utility Belt begins to beep again. Poison Ivy hears it. She turns just in time to see the Batarang spinning toward her. She ducks and the Batarang passes just over her head. Your presence has been revealed. And Poison Ivy still clutches the deadly detonator in her fist.

The report tells you that Mr. Freeze is threatening to freeze the city's water supply so that no water will flow through pipes anywhere in Gotham. Again, two potentially deadly crimes are happening at once! The city's power supply and water supply are both in danger! What do you do?

If you think you should rush off to the reservoir, go to Chapter 24.

If you think you should stay and battle Poison Ivy, go to Chapter 5.

16

You take the most direct route to get to Arkham Asylum, realizing that you've wasted too much time already. The answer clearly lies there, and the sooner you get there, the sooner you can clear up this mystery.

But anticipating the route you were going to take—the most direct route to Arkham—your four enemies lie in wait. When you reach a crossroads on the way to Arkham, Mr. Freeze, Riddler, Catwoman, and Poison Ivy are waiting for you. All their crimes, all their trickery, all their antics leading you on an endless, pointless chase, were just a big set-up.

They knew that sooner or later you would come to Arkham, and they guessed the route you would take. This whole mystery was one big trap, and now you've fallen into it.

Poison Ivy stings you with her pheromones and you fall into a daze; then Mr. Freeze encases you in ice with a blast from his Freeze Gun. All four enemies attack you at once, overwhelming you.

THE END

17

You track Mr. Freeze to a water park. There you capture him in your Batrope.

"I know where I can get some answers from you," you say to Mr. Freeze. "Let's go to Arkham. I'll put you into the same cell as the other Mr. Freeze, the guy I saw when I went there earlier. Then we'll figure out what's going on. We'll see who the true Freeze really is."

You lead the still-silent Mr. Freeze along, pulling on the Batrope as if it were a leash. You head back to the Batmobile to bring Freeze to Arkham. At the very least, he'll be back in the asylum where he belongs. But your genuine hope is that you'll find the answers you've been looking for there, with one of the four super-villains who have been leading you on this chase in tow.

"Come on!" you shout, realizing that Freeze is doing everything in his power to slow you down.

Without warning, Mr. Freeze stumbles and falls to the ground. His weight yanks the end of the Batrope from your hands. You spin around, ready to do battle, but before you can reach Freeze, he leans down toward his feet.

Even though his arms are pinned to his sides, he is still able to reach into his boot and pull out a miniature version of his Freeze Gun. First he blasts the Batrope, freezing, then shattering, the cable, freeing himself. Then he fires the weapon at you, stinging and numbing your legs.

You are momentarily frozen in place. But that's all the time Mr. Freeze needs. By the time your legs regain feeling, Freeze has disappeared again.

If you think you should chase after Mr. Freeze, go to Chapter 26.

If you think you should turn your attention to another super-villain, go to Chapter 42.

18

You decide to follow the clue and hurry to the textile factory. You certainly don't expect the Joker to be standing there waiting to be arrested. But you do hope that maybe you'll be able to find some additional clues to his actual whereabouts.

Slipping into the factory, you immediately spot several clues that were obviously left in plain sight for you to find. A stuffed cat's paw dangles from the ceiling.

Okay, Catwoman was here, or at least someone wants me to think she was.

One wall of the factory is covered with small pieces of paper. On each paper is a riddle.

One of the riddles reads: "I make you laugh. I make you cry. And you pay me to do it! What am I?"

Beside this riddle is a set of comedy and tragedy masks.

"Obviously, he means a theater," you say to yourself. "That seems to be where they want me to go next."

But once again you wonder if it's a trap, another step on this seemingly endless chase, or the real hideout where you might find the Joker.

If you think you should go to the sewer system, go to Chapter 43.

If you think you should go to the theater, go to Chapter 45.

19

I'm not letting her get away this time! I'll have to deal with whatever is going on at the water park later.

You fling your Batrope up to a flagpole near the top of the building. It wraps around the pole securely. Then you begin your climb up toward Catwoman, who smiles at you as she waves the sack of stolen jewels back and forth, baiting you to come and get her.

Higher and higher you climb, moving faster and faster. When you are one floor beneath Catwoman, she scrambles back onto the roof of the building. Reaching the roof a few seconds later, you vault up and onto its black tar surface, just in time to see Catwoman slip through the roof door.

You race across the roof, your strides as long as an Olympic sprinter's. You reach the door in seconds and dash down the stairs, taking three at a time.

At each turn in the staircase you catch a fleeting glimpse of Catwoman's black bodysuit zooming ahead of you.

Vaulting over the stair railing at the second floor, you drop two stories, pulling your arms close to your body, turning yourself into a human torpedo. You slip through the narrow opening that runs down the center of the staircase.

Hitting the floor in the lobby of the building, you allow your body to accordion into a crouch, to relieve the pressure on your knees and ankles. Straightening up, you look in every direction, but can catch no sign of Catwoman.

You race out the front door into the mob of people on the street.

"Where did Catwoman go?" you ask the police officer who is holding back the crowd.

"She didn't come out this way, Batman," he replies. "I haven't seen her since she went up onto the roof."

You turn and run back into the building, but the sinking feeling in your stomach tells you that you've lost her—again!

What do you do now?
Solve this puzzle to help
you decide what to do next.

Code Key

!=A, @=B, #=C,
$=D, %=E, ^=F,
&=G, *=H, Ω=I,
∑=J, +=K, [=L,
{=M,]=N, }=O,
>=P, <=Q, ?=R,
¢=S, £=T, ¤=U,
§=V, Δ=W,
©=X, €=Y, ◊=Z

SECRET CODE

*Use this Code Key to decode
this secret coded message:*

_ _ _ _ _ _ _ _ _ _ _
^ ? } ◊ %]   Δ ! £ % ?

_ _ _ _ _ _ _ _
Ω]   ¢ ¤ { { % ?

If you think you should go to the water park,
go to Chapter 9.

If you think you should go back to the Batcave to
figure out why criminals who should be in Arkham
Asylum are out in Gotham, go to Chapter 58.

20

It appears from the Batcomputer's analysis and from the map showing on its monitor that Poison Ivy may be lurking in the Gotham City Botanical Gardens.

Too easy, you think. *Too obvious. Or does that make it a perfect choice?*

As you think through the task of trying to stop two super-villains at once, you feel that some action is better than none. You return to the Batmobile and speed from the Batcave.

Because the Gotham Botanical Gardens is so obvious a choice, you fear a trap. Having fallen under the spell of Poison Ivy's pheromones before, you have no desire to be intoxicated by them ever again. With a small, self-contained breathing mask in your Utility Belt, you slip from the Batmobile and make your way around the high fence that surrounds the gardens. You keep your back against the fence.

Reaching a spot where trees outside the garden have overgrown the fence, you scramble up a tree and swing yourself from branch to branch. Peeking out from between two leaf-covered branches, you peer through binoculars into the lush gardens.

Visitors pack the place, admiring the beautiful flowers and trees. Using your binoculars' zoom technology, you gaze across the gardens to a dense, woods-like area. You recall coming here as a boy and pretending that you were in a forest, amazed that in the middle of bustling Gotham City you could lose yourself in a wooded enclave.

She would be too obvious out in the crowd, you think. *If she's here, the woods are where she'll be.*

You climb down the tree and continue around the outside of the gardens. Reaching the wooded section, you scramble over the fence and into the park.

The noise of the crowd is muffled as you enter the mini-forest. The daylight is also diminished by the thick grove of trees, making you feel more at home in the semi-darkness.

Reaching the largest tree, one with a thick trunk, you spot something strange—hinges on the bark. Apparently Poison Ivy has hollowed out the trunk and is hiding inside.

You sense an opportunity to take her by surprise and stop at least one of the two super-villains who have apparently escaped from Arkham.

If you think you should confront Poison Ivy right now, go to Chapter 40.

If you think you should change your plan and go after Catwoman, go to Chapter 19.

21

The dock, you think. *I'll catch up with the Riddler at the dock.*

With that in mind you rush to the Gotham City waterfront but find it deserted.

I didn't expect the Riddler to be waiting for me out in the open.

You search the area near the dock but still find no one. Slipping into a warehouse that backs up against the river, you switch on your fingerlight, sweeping its white LED beam across the darkened warehouse. Rats scurry across the filthy wooden floor, startled by the piercing bright light. Pigeons drop from the rafters, swooping past your head.

Still, no sign of the Riddler.

Emerging from the warehouse, out into the misty afternoon, you step onto the dock to take a closer look at the river.

THOOM!

Your first footstep sets off a small, weight-sensitive explosive. The dock explodes, torn to pieces. You plunge into the dark, cold river.

THE END

22

You increase your speed, climbing rapidly, hoping to catch Catwoman before she can make her escape. Hands flashing in a blur, feet barely touching its slick glass surface, you scramble up the side of the building.

Again, you hear a noise. This time it's right above your head. It's a dull, scratching sound—one you've heard before.

A figure suddenly appears above you, blocking the moon from your view.

"Hello, Batman!" Catwoman purrs softly. "I can't say that I'm surprised. I've been expecting you!"

Something's wrong! you think. *Why would Catwoman just be waiting here to be caught? I smell a trap.*

You turn to race back down the building to give yourself a moment to regroup, to think, to find a way out of what you are now certain is a trap.

SNAP!

A horrible snapping sound explodes right above you. Whipping your head around, you look back up in time to see a thick rope net dropping toward you. Shifting your weight to one side, you push off with your feet, launching yourself away from the building, hoping to swing clear of the plunging net.

You swing away from the building on your Batrope.

I'll make it...just barely, but I'll—

THWAPT!

A heavy blanket of rope slams into you, knocking you from the Batrope and catching you in its chunky, tangled web. You smash your face into the netting, then roll over onto your side, desperately trying to break free.

Flipping yourself around onto your back, you realize that there is no way out. You are trapped.

Catwoman stares down at you and laughs—a demented, sickening cackle—as you dangle, swaying in the gentle breeze.

"I'll CAT–ch up with you later, Batman," she screeches. Then she turns and scampers away, leaving you trapped, thirty stories above the pavement!

THE END

23

The Joker himself is a hologram! He's not really there, and the holo projection is so good even his henchmen never realized it.

Suddenly a SWAT team of police officers bursts into the room. You had clued them in to your plan, hoping they could help you catch the Joker. You didn't get him, but the SWAT team does round up his henchmen. Before too long these four will be safely back in Arkham where they belong.

With the police in control of situation, you take off, fleeing the sewer.

As you speed home in the Batmobile, you think to yourself, *I'd better call Lucius and tell him that we are definitely NOT investing in that technology company!*

CONGRATULATIONS!
You've captured the super-villains!

24

You race to the reservoir and discover that Mr. Freeze has frozen the entire Gotham City water supply and is now standing on the ice. You quickly scale the outside of the dam that holds the water, intending to grab Mr. Freeze's Freeze Gun. Taking away his most potent weapon will make Freeze easier to stop.

But Mr. Freeze spots you climbing up the face of the dam and fires a path of ice down the wall. The ice passes under your fingers and your boots and you begin to slide downward. Spinning in mid-air, you manage to regain a grip on the dam's surface, but Mr. Freeze prepares to fire again.

Suddenly the receiver on your Utility Belt sounds. An urgent message comes in: Catwoman has broken into the Gotham City Museum. It is the height of tourist season and the museum attracts many visitors. Hundreds of people could be in danger. Is stopping Mr. Freeze more urgent than catching Catwoman?

UNSCRAMBLE

Unscramble the following words and write them in the spaces. Then read down the circled column to get a clue as to which villain poses an immediate threat to the city.

EDENDF   __ __ __ __ __ __

OTRFN   __ __ __ __ __

TWE   __ __ __

TAEWR   __ __ __ __ __

IZP   __ __ __

RETAHB   __ __ __ __ __ __

. . . .

If you think you should stay and fight Mr. Freeze,
go to Chapter 10.

If you think you should go to stop Catwoman,
go to Chapter 4.

25

"Here's our chance to find out who is in those cells," Dr. Arkham says. "Come with me."

You follow Dr. Arkham to Catwoman's cell. She is still sitting there, staring right at you.

"How can she be here and also be at that factory?" Dr. Arkham asks. "They both appear to really be Catwoman."

"Can I take a look at the asylum's records for the past few days, Doctor?" you ask.

"Of course, Batman. Follow me."

You hurry back to Dr. Arkham's office and flip through the asylum's operating logs for the past several days. These records keep track of all the goings-on in the building.

As you flip from page to page, something strange suddenly jumps out at you.

"Now this is odd," you say, pointing to an entry in the log. "It appears that a brief power outage took place a few days ago in the middle of the night."

"That happens from time to time," Dr. Arkham explains. "It's not particularly unusual."

"Yes, I know," you reply. "But this is somewhat strange. It seems that at the very moment the power was restored, a huge power surge was recorded. What could have caused that enormous jump in power?"

"I don't know, Batman. That is curious. Our power usage tends to remain fairly steady."

"This could be the clue we've been looking for," you say.

But what does it mean?

Solve the puzzle to find out.

After solving the puzzle, if you think you should run a check of the electrical systems at Arkham, go to Chapter 54.

After solving the puzzle, if you think you should continue to search Arkham's records for more clues, go to Chapter 3.

WORD SEARCH

Find and circle the following words. Then list the remaining letters (those not circled) to reveal a clue.

JAIL
CELL
DOOR
KEY
BLOCK
LOCK
TRAP

A	N	J	E	W	P
T	R	A	P	I	E
C	E	I	O	F	E
C	E	L	L	Q	U
I	P	D	O	O	R
B	L	O	C	K	M
E	N	T	K	E	Y

__ ____ _____ ___

_____

26

You pursue, following closely, unsure if following was a wise decision. Your answer comes swiftly and definitively. Steel walls drop down on all sides of you. You are trapped inside a thick metal box. Before you have time to toss a Batrope and climb out the top, another steel plate slams down, sealing you inside.

You hear the sound of gears grinding. Then the walls begin to close in on you. You try desperately to get out, but you realize quickly that there is no escape. No trick or gimmick, no device in your Utility Belt, can help you now.

You have been defeated.

THE END

27

This is bigger than just the Riddler, you think. *And he hasn't actually committed a crime—other than somehow breaking out of prison, of course. No, I need to get to the bottom of this whole situation.*

You return to the Batcave, thinking about Catwoman, Poison Ivy, Mr. Freeze, and the Riddler. They all seem to have escaped at once, yet no one at Arkham has contacted you.

Perhaps the time has come for me to take a trip to Arkham to investigate just what's going on.

As you prepare to go to Arkham, the Batcomputer signals an alarm just as it did when the Riddler's first riddle came in. You rush to the screen and see a flashing message. It's from the Riddler!

Again the Riddler has hacked into the Batcave's main computer. But once more, there is no time to do a full system check on the Batcomputer. The flashing message icon on the screen changes into another riddle.

Only this time the riddle comes in the form of a puzzle you have to solve.

WORD SEARCH

Find and circle all the following words. Then list the remaining letters (those not circled) to solve the Riddler's puzzle and discover a clue to everything that's been going on.

CRIME   RIDDLE   VICTIM   ESCAPE

C G O T O A

R I D D L E

I R K H A M

M I T C I V

E S C A P E

____ ____ _____

If you think you should go back out after the Riddler,
go to Chapter 38.

If you think you should go right to Arkham to
investigate, go to Chapter 28.

28

You decide that the answers you've been looking for will be found at Arkham. You also realize that your enemies know that at some point you will go to Arkham to investigate. And so, fearing that they might be waiting for you if you travel there via the main route, you take a back road known only to a few people.

You steer the Batmobile along narrow, winding dirt roads, tracing the outskirts of Gotham. As you near your destination, you cut the Batmobile's engines and glide to a stop at the rear of Arkham Asylum.

Slipping from the Batmobile, you look up at the asylum's tall Gothic spires. You know that Dr. Jeremiah Arkham, who runs the institution, is doing groundbreaking medical work.

You reach the highly fortified rear entrance to

the asylum. Stepping up to the thick steel door, you remove your right glove and press your thumb against a scanner. The blinking red light on the scanner switches from red to green. You open the door and slip inside. Had your thumbprint not been on file, alarms would have sounded and a large steel gate would have slid out, trapping you inside.

You move down a short corridor. At the end of the hallway you reach a door. You enter a five-digit code into a keypad. A monitor blazes to life, revealing the face of Dr. Jeremiah Arkham.

"Batman!" Dr. Arkham exclaims. "What brings you here?"

"We need to talk, Dr. Arkham," you reply.

"Of course, of course—come in."

A buzzer sounds, signaling that Dr. Arkham has unlocked the door. You slip through and make your way to Dr. Arkham's office.

"I'd like to check on the status of a few of your inmates," you explain. You think it odd that Dr. Arkham seems to have no idea that some of his most dangerous patients have apparently escaped.

"Certainly, Batman. Which ones?"

"Catwoman, Poison Ivy, the Riddler, and Mr. Freeze," you reply.

Dr. Arkham nods, then grabs a set of keys and leads you to the maximum security area. First stop, the Riddler's cell.

You peer through thick steel bars and see the Riddler sitting in his cell, writing in a notebook. He looks up, stares right out at you, then lets out a shrieking cackle.

How can this be? you wonder. *I just saw him out and about in Gotham.*

You next visit the cell of Poison Ivy. She too is there, grooming a vining plant. She turns to look at you and reaches out a hand, her long, green fingernails stretching toward you.

Again, a criminal you just battled on the outside.

Mr. Freeze's cell is next. He is there, but he doesn't even bother to look up at you.

Lastly, you visit Catwoman's cell. By now you are not surprised to find her in her cell as well. She looks at you, then wags a finger at you suggestively.

"I've seen enough," you say, turning and heading back to Dr. Arkham's office. Once there, you fill him in on the activities of the four criminals who are clearly still behind bars.

"But how can that be?" Dr. Arkham asks.

"I'm thinking now that several copycats may have been dressing up as these four, committing these crimes and leading me on a chase," you explain. "It's the first and most logical explanation I can come up with, now that I see them all still here."

"I see," Dr. Arkham replies.

"But now my task becomes even more difficult," you point out. "Now I've not only got to stop these fakes, who also seem to display the abilities of the real villains, but I've got to figure out who is really behind this recent crime wave, pretending to be some of my most dangerous enemies. Thank you, Dr. Arkham. Good-bye."

Returning to the Batmobile, you speed away from Arkham, retracing the back roads you took to get there. You ponder your next move, but you don't have long to wait.

Three reports come in all at once—Catwoman has broken into the Gotham City Museum; Poison Ivy has staged an attack at a power plant; and Mr. Freeze has frozen the water in the Gotham City reservoir that supplies the city with its drinking water.

Code Key

!=A, @=B, #=C,
$=D, %=E, ^=F,
&=G, *=H, Ω=I,
∑=J, +=K, [=L,
{=M,]=N, }=O,
>=P, <=Q, ?=R,
¢=S, £=T, ¤=U,
§=V, Δ=W,
©=X, €=Y, ◊=Z

SECRET CODE

Use this Code Key to decode this secret coded message:

$$\overline{\ }\ \overline{\ }\ \overline{\ }\quad \overline{\ }\ \overline{\ }\ \overline{\ }\ \overline{\ }\ \overline{\ }$$

! [[£ * ? % %

$$\overline{\ }\ \overline{\ }\ \overline{\ }\ \overline{\ }\ \overline{\ }\ \overline{\ }\ \overline{\ }\quad \overline{\ }\ \overline{\ }\ \overline{\ }\quad \overline{\ }\ \overline{\ }\ \overline{\ }\ \overline{\ }$$

! £ £ ! # + ¢   ! ? %   ? % ! [

If you think you should go to the Gotham City Museum to investigate Catwoman, go to Chapter 4.

If you think you should go to the power plant to investigate Poison Ivy, go to Chapter 15.

If you think you should go to the reservoir to investigate Mr. Freeze, go to Chapter 24.

29

You peer through the window of the factory, but see no sign of Catwoman. No surprise there. She would not make herself obvious to you. Just not her style.

Still, climbing right through the window that she might actually want you to come through is not the best idea either. You move to the next window, farther away from the street. This one is shut tightly. Struggling to get it open would alert Catwoman to your presence.

No, you've got to get inside and announce your arrival all in one quick motion. Firing a grapnel hook to the floor above, you swing backward on the line, then crash feet-first right through the window.

KA-RASH!

Landing on the floor in a spray of wood and glass, you look around quickly but see no sign of Catwoman.

Suddenly the factory explodes!

THOOM!

It collapses all around you.

THE END

30

Speeding through the streets of Gotham in the Batmobile, you arrive at the smoldering wreckage of the chemical factory. Pulling on a gas mask hooked up to a special breathing apparatus, you slip through a broken window and head inside.

Peering though the smoke and fumes, you see firefighters still hard at work, keeping the toxic blaze under control.

Ironic, you think, *that if this is the work of Poison Ivy, she would probably claim to have done it in the name of environmentalism. Yet this blast has released a ton of toxic smoke into the air.*

That's when you see it. A vague green shape flickering in and out of view as the smoke drifts past your eyes. Maneuvering through the smoky chaos, you reach the far wall. There, you spy a thin piece of vine clinging to the charred wall.

Poison Ivy! So I was right. Lifting your breathing mask, you quickly sniff the piece of vine. The unmistakable odor of Poison Ivy's pheromones floods your nostrils. You begin to feel dizzy. But having dealt with this powerful, mind-controlling concoction many times before, you quickly press the breathing mask against your mouth and nose and take several deep breaths of pure oxygen. Then you cut a sample of the vine and place it into a plastic container, which you seal with an airtight closure.

Your head clears, but now you are certain that this explosion was no accident. This was most definitely the work of Poison Ivy.

Again, the impossible seems to have come true, you think. Like Catwoman, Poison Ivy is also safely behind bars at Arkham Asylum. You put her there as well!

If you think you should go to the Batcave, go to Chapter 31.

If you think you should try to find Poison Ivy, go to Chapter 20.

31

Hurrying back to the Batmobile, you speed toward the Batcave. Your mind races with the realization that you now have two of your greatest enemies to stop—at the same time.

More troubling is the fact that both these criminals are supposed to be locked behind bars at a top-level maximum security facility. How could both of them have escaped…without anyone noticing? Certainly if there had been some kind of breakout, you would have been the first to have heard about it. It just doesn't add up. And you hate it when things don't add up.

Racing through the maze of underground tunnels leading to the Batcave, you screech to a stop, then leap from the Batmobile's cockpit-like driver's seat. You quickly input into the Batcomputer all the information you have gathered about both Catwoman's recent cat burglary capers and Poison Ivy's attack on the chemical factory.

You set the Batcomputer to work correlating the locations of Catwoman's recent rash of robberies. You also program in all the details of your investigation at the chemical factory, including the sample of the green vine you took.

You pace back and forth, using all your years of crime-fighting experience as well as your own finely honed mind to try to put the pieces together.

Suddenly the Batcomputer signals you that it has come to some conclusions, or at least it has analyzed the information you put in deeply enough so it can offer you something helpful.

You hurry back and look at the Batcomputer's large computer screen. The Batcomputer has come up with a possible location for each of the two super-villains. But you can't be in two places at once.

Which criminal should you go after?

If you reach Poison Ivy first, go to Chapter 20.

If you reach Catwoman first, go to Chapter 14.

32

You turn the holo-device over and over in your hands. You realize that further study is needed.

"May I take this with me?" you ask Dr. Arkham. "I can analyze it in the Batcave."

"Of course, Batman. Anything to help. But who could be behind all this? Who has this level of technology that's so good it fooled both of us?"

"That's what I hope to discover," you say, rushing from Dr. Arkham's office.

Retracing your steps to the Batmobile, you speed back through the woods, hugging the back roads, zooming back to the Batcave as fast as your sleek machine will move. This is the first real break you've gotten in this case. You want to jump on this lead while the trail is still warm.

Back in the Batcave, you begin your research. You take the holo-projector apart and scan each piece into the Batcomputer, analyzing its blueprints and specifications.

Hmm, you think, studying the data. *Something about this is familiar.*

You run a comparison of the specs with the huge database on the Batcomputer. After a few minutes you are frustrated to discover that no match comes up.

"Where have I seen these specs before?" you wonder aloud. Then it dawns on you. Perhaps you didn't see them as Batman. Maybe you saw them as Bruce Wayne.

You quickly network the Batcomputer into the main computer of Wayne Enterprises. When the secure link is established, you run the comparison of the specs again.

This time, you get a match.

The specs for the holo projection system you took from Arkham exactly match the ones for the new communications device that was supposed to revolutionize video games—the very system you've been talking with Lucius about.

That's the connection! you realize. *No wonder the CEO wanted to remain in the shadows. Apparently new video games are not the only thing this technology can do. Helping criminals escape from maximum security facilities seems to be another app.*

At that moment, a message pops up on the Batcomputer. Catwoman and the Riddler have just teamed up to rob a penthouse art gallery of its treasures. At least now you know that they are the real Catwoman and Riddler.

If you think you should go after the super-villains, go to Chapter 47.

If you think you should try to track down the person behind the holo scheme, go to Chapter 56.

33

You decide that Freeze may just hold the answer to this entire mystery. Searching the area around the reservoir, you find faint footsteps outlined in a thin coating of ice. You smile, thinking that Mr. Freeze left behind the most simple, basic clue—footprints. But this means that you'll have to track Freeze on foot.

You follow the footprints, but they grow more and more faint, the farther away from the reservoir you get. Tracking the prints, you soon find yourself near the edge of downtown Gotham.

Another chase through the heart of the city. Great! you think. At that moment you spot Mr. Freeze. He's about to enter a crowded downtown street. You realize that any battle with him would endanger innocent bystanders.

Picking up your pace, you approach Mr. Freeze with utmost stealth. Snatching a Batarang with a Batrope attached to it, you fling it toward Freeze.

Before he is even aware that you or the weapon is there, the Batarang has wrapped the Batrope around Freeze, pinning his arms to his sides. Maintaining a firm grip on the other end of the line, you yank him toward you. Then you pin him against the side of a building.

"You're going to talk," you snarl at him. "Right now!"

Mr. Freeze looks away.

"What is going on?" you demand. "How did you and the others get out of Arkham! Speak! Now!"

But Mr. Freeze remains tight-lipped.

Suddenly a message comes into the communicator on your Utility Belt.

Another crime? What now?

The message turns out to be another riddle from the Riddler. But this time you don't need to decode it. You just need to figure out what the Riddler, in his demented mind, means by it. The riddle reads:

"You belong in Arkham."

If you think you should bring Mr. Freeze back to Arkham, go to Chapter 17.

If you think you should try to find the Riddler, go to Chapter 42.

34

You believe that the answer to the riddle is "doctor." Knowing the way the Riddler's mind works, you hurry to the Gotham Medical Center.

You approach the hospital's main security desk.

"Batman!" the security guard exclaims in surprise. "Is everything all right?"

"That's what I was about to ask you," you say. "Any sign of trouble? Any unusual activity?"

"Not that I saw, Batman," the guard replies.

You nod, then hurry into the building.

His riddle was so obvious that I'm sure the Riddler would not pick an actual doctor's office as a place to confront me. I'm thinking the roof, since he knows I would always look there. Trying your best to keep out of sight, you join several hospital orderlies in the service elevator.

"Batman!" says one of the orderlies. "Are you sick? Or injured?"

"Never better," you reply, as everyone else steps off the car at the ninth floor. You ride up to the tenth floor alone, then rush from the elevator to the door that leads to the building's roof.

You step out onto the roof. Wind whips your cape behind you as you glance in all directions. No sign of anyone.

Stepping out from behind a huge air vent, the Riddler lets out a cackle.

"Riddler!" you shout. "I thought you'd be here."

Again he laughs at you, doubling himself over, snorting and howling in derision.

"How did you and the others get out of Arkham?" you demand. "What kind of trick is this?" You grow angrier by the second and more and more frustrated at the seeming ease with which four of your worst enemies have gotten out of the maximum security facility—a place where you had assumed they would spend years safely behind bars.

The Riddler simply emits his demented laugh again. Then he turns and runs away. You follow him down the stairs and out of the hospital, doctors and patients scattering before you.

The Riddler hits the street, and you realize that he is heading in the direction of the Gotham waterfront.

If you think you should follow the Riddler, go to Chapter 21.

If you think you should go back to the Batcave to try to make sense of all this, go to Chapter 27.

35

You dash across the roof and peer down, just in time to see Catwoman slipping back through a window.

She's going back inside! you think. *She's not trying to get away—she's intent on leading me on another chase. This time through the museum!*

Scrambling back over the edge of the roof, you slip through a window on the opposite side from the one Catwoman just used. Once inside the museum, you spot her in a gallery of priceless ancient pottery.

You dash across the gleaming marble floor and catch up to Catwoman within seconds.

"How did you and the others get out of Arkham?" you demand. "I know you are in league with them. Your timing is all too perfect."

"Shhh!" Catwoman replies, putting a gloved finger to her lips. "It's a secret."

Then, as if to test you, she intentionally knocks over display stand after display stand, sending a series of antiquities into your path. You dive after a vase, which you place gently on the floor, only to scramble to your feet in order to catch a tiny pre-Columbian bowl just inches from the floor.

This is all a game to her, you think, reaching out with one hand to snag an ancient platter, while grabbing another vase a fraction of a second before it would have shattered into shards.

Having rescued the priceless pottery, you realize that you have lost sight of Catwoman. She remedies that by sticking her head around an archway leading to the medieval exhibit.

"I missed you, Batman!" she coos.

You run into that gallery but are immediately assaulted by a huge suit of armor that tumbles toward you, sword-first. You dive out of the way and regain your feet in time to see Catwoman jump onto a window ledge. She turns and waves goodbye, then springs out of the window.

If you think you should follow Catwoman out the window, go to Chapter 26.

If you think you should let Catwoman get away and hurry to the power plant to stop Poison Ivy from blowing it up, go to Chapter 5.

36

Your gut instinct is to rush off, change into Batman, and speed to the chemical factory.

"An early investigation of the incident indicates that the explosion was an accident and not a terrorist attack, as some first feared," continues the newsfeed voice.

"Sounds like an accident," you say to Lucius, answering his unspoken question. Then you turn back to researching the communication company.

"This is so peculiar, Lucius," you say. "The more I dig around, the less I seem to be able to find out about this company. It doesn't even list the CEO's name. As tempting as this new technology sounds, I'm uneasy investing in a company when I can't find a single word about its CEO."

"I'm with you, Bruce," Lucius says. "The worth of a company is directly related to the quality of its

CEO. I think we should dig a bit deeper, maybe call some of our friends in the high-tech communications sector to—"

The news monitor begins beeping again.

"Breaking news on that explosion at the Gotham Chemical factory," the reporter says. "Police have now concluded that the explosion may have been a guerrilla-style terrorist attack deliberately perpetrated against a company targeted as a big polluter."

You look at Lucius. "Sounds like the work of Poison Ivy," you say. "Not an accident after all."

If you think you should change into Batman and investigate the explosion in the chemical factory, go to Chapter 30.

If you think you should go to the Batcave, go to Chapter 31.

37

Is the "sewer" clue a trick? Should I look elsewhere? I've got to find out for sure.

You head down into the sewer and come to a locked door. *I know better than to burst right through this door.* Climbing to the catwalk above, you toss a Batarang that embeds itself in the door. Then you yank hard on the line and pull it open.

KA-THOOM!

A huge explosion rips the door from its hinges. You duck away from the smoke and debris. Grabbing your Batrope, you swing into the room, startling Catwoman, Poison Ivy, the Riddler, Mr. Freeze, and the Joker himself!

Go to Chapter 59.

38

You decide to go after the Riddler. Within moments of driving out of the Batcave, you spot a giant question mark spray-painted on the side of a building. Screeching to a stop, you leap out of the Batmobile and search the area near the building.

You find no sign of the Riddler.

You spy another giant question mark covering an advertising billboard. Hopping back into the Batmobile, you speed down the street.

You get out to investigate, and again you find no sign of the Riddler. This pursuit is starting to take on the feel of this entire situation—one wild goose chase after another, one dead end after another.

Still, something tells you to go on; something tells you that the answer to this whole thing might just lie with the Riddler. You drive on, eyes peeled. A few minutes later you discover yet another question mark. This one is painted on the side of a large warehouse.

Leaving the Batmobile a block away, you creep silently toward the warehouse. Tossing a Batrope up to the roof, you scramble up the side of the warehouse until you come to a window. Peering through the cracked, grime-covered glass, you can barely believe your eyes. There stands the Riddler, staring right at you!

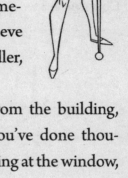

Pushing yourself back away from the building, you tense your leg muscles, as you've done thousands of times before. Then you swing at the window, feet first.

CRASH!

You explode through the pane, sending shards of glass and splintered pieces of window frame spraying into the building. Landing in a crouched, ready position, you whip out a Batarang, poised to throw.

"It's over, Riddler!" you shout. "You're coming with me and you're going to give me some answers!"

But the Riddler just leans back, lets out a shrieking, maniacal laugh, and runs from the warehouse.

If you think you should go after the Riddler, go to Chapter 53.

If you think you should go to Arkham Asylum for answers instead of chasing the Riddler, go to Chapter 28.

39

You bolt up the side of the building, increasing your speed, moving instinctively, sensing your enemy. Then you suddenly stop.

Something's not right here, you think. *I know Catwoman all too well, and she wouldn't make herself known to me, then just sit there waiting to be caught. I smell a trap!*

Using your momentum, you swing out sideways on your Batrope, floating around the corner of the building. Your feet land on a window with a gentle, almost imperceptible tap.

Silently you speed up to the roof of the building. There, you see Catwoman peering down over the edge of the roof toward where you had been climbing just moments earlier.

She is holding a release lever attached to a thick rope net dangling from the roof.

So that was her game, you think, vaulting up onto the roof. *Maybe I can turn the tables on this trap.*

Swiftly and stealthily you pull a Batarang from your Utility Belt. As you draw back your arm to fling the weapon at Catwoman, your boot scrapes against the rough roofing material. Catwoman spins toward you.

"Clever, the way you outsmarted my trap, Batman," Catwoman says. "But not clever enough!"

You toss your Batarang, but Catwoman slips over the edge of the roof, carrying a sack of stolen jewelry, just as the Batarang passes above her head.

I'm not going to lose her now that I've found her, you think as you dash across the rooftop. You scramble over the edge of the roof close on Catwoman's heels.

Catwoman climbs down a rope ladder that hangs along the side of the building. You drop a Batrope down the same side and race down after her. Catwoman reaches the sidewalk just seconds before you. She runs at top speed, clutching the stolen jewels tightly.

Just as you reach the ground you see Catwoman duck into an alley. Her footsteps go silent.

Where did she go? you wonder, pausing at the entrance to the alley.

WORD SEARCH

Find and circle all the following words. Then list the remaining letters (those not circled) to reveal a clue.

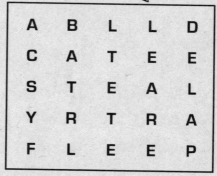

BAT

CAT

FREED

STEAL

FLEE

A	B	L	L	D
C	A	T	E	E
S	T	E	A	L
Y	R	T	R	A
F	L	E	E	P

_____ _____

• • • • • • • •

After solving the puzzle, if you think you should go into the alley, go to Chapter 51.

If you think you should give up the chase right here, go to Chapter 12.

40

You quietly creep up to the tree. Placing tiny amounts of plastic explosives onto the two hinges, you then fling a Batrope to a branch above and scramble up the line. Hanging upside down, you detonate the two small charges.

BOOM!

A small explosion pops the hinges off the door, which is made out of a section of the tree bark. You slowly lower yourself toward the opening in the tree trunk. Looking in, you see a tiny makeshift lab—but no sign of Poison Ivy.

"Looking for someone, Batman?" says a voice from above you.

You spin around and find yourself face to face with Poison Ivy. It was a trap, and you fell right into it!

Dropping to the ground, you roll out of the way. Poison Ivy leaps down beside you. She steps forward, ready to attack.

UNSCRAMBLE

Unscramble the following words and write them in the spaces. Then read down the circled column to learn what Poison Ivy plans to use to fight you.

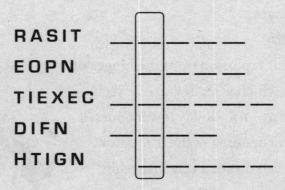

RASIT _ _ _ _ _

EOPN _ _ _ _

TIEXEC _ _ _ _ _ _

DIFN _ _ _ _

HTIGN _ _ _ _ _

If you think you should meet Poison Ivy's attack directly, go to Chapter 52.

If you think you should retreat and go after Catwoman instead, go to Chapter 14.

41

You finally know that the Joker has been behind all this. But now the hard work really begins. You must search Gotham City, inch by inch, checking all the various hideouts you know the Joker has.

But where to begin?

UNSCRAMBLE

Unscramble the following words, then read down the circled column to figure out where you should go next.

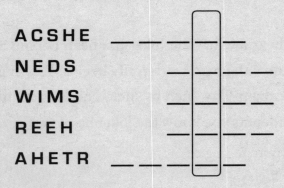

ACSHE   __ __ __ __ __

NEDS   __ __ __ __

WIMS   __ __ __ __

REEH   __ __ __ __

AHETR   __ __ __ __ __

If you think you should try to stop Catwoman and the Riddler before going after the Joker, go to Chapter 11.

If you think you should go to the Joker's hideout in the sewers of Gotham, go to Chapter 6.

42

"'You belong in Arkham,'" you say, repeating the Riddler's riddle aloud.

You wonder what the Riddler could mean by that. Does he really think that you should be put into the hospital for the criminally insane? Is he just taunting you? Does he think he's insulting you?

That's not the Riddler's style. He always has a double meaning in his riddles.

"'You belong in Arkham,'" you say again.

Then it dawns on you.

Is he trying to tell me that in order to solve this mystery I belong in Arkham, meaning that I should go there to unravel this case?

Then you wonder why the Riddler would give you what could turn out to be a very helpful clue. Or maybe it isn't helpful at all.

Perhaps you have already learned everything there is to learn at Arkham and, by following his advice, you'd be running off on another fruitless chase, wasting more time, allowing the four criminals on the loose to do more harm, and moving even further from the truth.

You continue to ponder the riddle.

Code Key

!=A, @=B, #=C,
$=D, %=E, ^=F,
&=G, *=H, Ω=I,
∑=J, +=K, [=L,
{=M,]=N, }=O,
>=P, <=Q, ?=R,
¢=S, £=T, ¤=U,
§=V, Δ=W,
©=X, ϵ=Y, ◊=Z

SECRET CODE

Use this Code Key to decode this secret coded message:

_ _ _ _ _ _   _ _   _ _ _ _ _ _

!] ¢ Δ % ?   ! £   ! ? + * ! {

If you think you should go back to Arkham, go to Chapter 48.

If you think you should pursue another super-villain, go to Chapter 8.

43

Down you go into the dank, stinking Gotham City sewer system. You've been down in these tunnels before. Parts of this seemingly endless maze seem familiar, while you feel that in others you could get lost for days.

You hear a noise…a splashing sound. Pressing your back against the wall, you wait, hoping to catch one or more of your adversaries. But no luck—it's just several rats scurrying past. You continue.

Examining the cement walls as you go, you keep your eyes peeled in the dark for anything unusual. In a tiny offshoot of a service tunnel you see the faint outline of a door. Only the most perceptive detective would have even noticed that there was a door there. It's worth trying. Or is it?

Solve the puzzle on the next page to help you decide what to do next.

Code Key

!=A, @=B, #=C, $=D,
%=E, ^=F, &=G, *=H,
Ω=I, ∑=J, +=K, [=L, {=M,
]=N, }=O, >=P, <=Q, ?=R,
¢=S, £=T, ¤=U, §=V,
Δ=W, ©=X, €=Y, ◊=Z

SECRET CODE

Use this Code Key to decode this secret coded message:

$\underline{\$} \ \underline{!} \ \underline{]} \ \underline{\&} \ \underline{\%} \ \underline{?}$ $\underline{[} \ \underline{¤} \ \underline{?} \ \underline{+} \ \underline{¢}$

$\underline{@} \ \underline{\%} \ \underline{*} \ \underline{Ω} \ \underline{]} \ \underline{\$}$ $\underline{£} \ \underline{*} \ \underline{\%}$ $\underline{\$} \ \underline{\}} \ \underline{\}} \ \underline{?}$

If you think you should burst through the door,
go to Chapter 50.

If you think you should try something more subtle,
go to Chapter 37.

44

The only reason you can think of for the Joker to leave such an obvious clue is if there is a trap waiting for you at the textile factory. You stick with your original hunch and head down into the sewers of Gotham, where you have confronted the Joker in several hideouts over the years.

But you're not quite sure where to begin. Solve the maze on the next page for a clue.

If you go to the right-hand exit, go to Chapter 18.

If you go to the left-hand exit, go to Chapter 43.

45

I doubt the Joker would choose the movie theater at the mall, you think. *Not his style. I bet he means the old abandoned theater downtown.*

You decide to go to the old theater, believing that another clue awaits you there. And you are not disappointed.

Fearing a trap if you walk right through the front door leading in from the dilapidated lobby, you scoot around to the backstage entrance. But, once again, it seems that the Joker is one step ahead of you.

As you step through the back entrance, you trip over something. Hitting the floor, rolling over, and springing back to your feet, you see what it was you just tripped over—a Gotham City sewer cover. Sticking out from under the sewer cover is a piece of paper. Lifting the cover and snatching the paper, you see that it is a message of some kind. But the meaning of the message is not clear.

You must solve this puzzling message to determine your next step.

HIDDEN MESSAGE

Find the hidden message in the following sentence:

MEND STITCH SEW ERASE PATTERN

If you think you should force your way into the Joker's sewer hideout, go to Chapter 50.

If you think you should try something else, go to Chapter 37.

46

Pulling out a crime scene kit from your Utility Belt, you chip off a piece of the ice from the frozen slide and begin a chemical analysis.

While you are waiting for the results, you hear a strange sound. Or rather you experience a weird silence. A moment earlier the sound of rushing water filled the air from all the various slides and rides around the park. Now, one by one they are going silent.

BING!

Your crime scene kit signals that it has finished its analysis. The chemical formulation of the ice is a familiar one that unfortunately you have dealt with before. There's no doubt left. This is the work of Mr. Freeze! The chemical signature shows that the water has been altered by the power of Mr. Freeze's Freeze Gun.

"Looking for someone, Batman?" a voice booms out suddenly.

You turn and spot Mr. Freeze with his Freeze Gun a short distance away.

Solve this puzzle to help you decide what to do next.

HIDDEN MESSAGE

Find the hidden message in the following sentence:

If you think you should chase Mr. Freeze, go to Chapter 13.

If you think you should continue to try to figure out why all these villains are free, go to Chapter 7.

47

Now that you know that the criminals are indeed who they appear to be, you take off after Catwoman and the Riddler.

You race to the tall building that houses the penthouse art gallery in the posh section of downtown Gotham City. Once there, you dash into the building only to discover that the power system for the elevator has been cut off.

Guess I'll reach the roof my usual way, you think, *firing a Batrope and starting the long climb up. It would be nice if one of these days an elevator actually worked.*

As you approach the roof of the high-rise, you hear the unmistakable sound of helicopter blades whirring. Leaning back while still maintaining a firm grip on your Batrope, you catch a glimpse of a large painting being lifted up into the hovering chopper.

Gotta move faster!

You increase your pace, practically running up the side of the sleek glass building. When you are almost at the top, you hear a communications device buzz. But it is not the device on your Utility Belt. It's Bruce Wayne's cell phone!

Lucius. Great timing.

"Lucius, I'm a bit busy at the moment," you say, speaking on the hands-free device as you shimmy up the skyscraper, hand over hand.

"You're going to want to see this," Lucius replies. "I've found some important information about that video game company we were looking at. I think I might have even figured out who the CEO is."

If you think you should go meet with Lucius as Bruce Wayne, go to Chapter 56.

If you think you should continue to pursue Catwoman and the Riddler, go to Chapter 55.

48

You realize that going back to Arkham gives you the best chance to finally solve this mystery. Once again, you take the winding back route through the wooded sections on the outskirts of Gotham to keep your journey hidden from your enemies.

Arriving at the rear entrance to the asylum, you once again press your thumb against the scanner. The door opens and you hurry inside.

Moving down the short hallway, you enter the five-digit code into the keypad. A few minutes later you are meeting Dr. Jeremiah Arkham in his office.

"Do you have new information, Batman?" Dr. Arkham asks.

"Since I met with you, I have had additional confrontations with all four criminals," you explain. "In addition, several of the crimes took place simultaneously, so if this was a case of copycats, there would have to be a bunch of them. Everything I've seen and discovered suggests that the four who are out there are the real super-villains. Which makes me wonder just who is being held here in your cells."

Before Dr. Arkham can reply, the communicator on your Utility Belt starts beeping. You receive a message that Catwoman has been spotted near an abandoned factory, carrying the Cat's-Eye Diamond she stole from the museum.

If you think you should continue your investigation with Dr. Arkham, go to Chapter 25.

If you think you should go to the abandoned factory to pursue Catwoman, go to Chapter 29.

49

You follow Poison Ivy as your frustration level continues to grow. You need answers and none of the criminals you've been pursuing has been providing any.

You catch a glimpse of Poison Ivy heading to a residential section of Gotham City. You see her leaping to the rooftop of a nearby apartment building—territory in which you feel completely comfortable. You follow her to the rooftop.

But Poison Ivy turns out to be surprisingly quick. She scampers over the roof, leaps across an alley, and lands on the far roof without missing a stride.

You do the same.

This chase continues, building after building, until finally you spot her ducking into a rooftop stairwell.

Good, you think. *I've got her!*

WORD SEARCH

Find and circle all the following words. Then list the remaining letters (those not circled) to reveal a clue.

DOOR   POISON   OPEN   IVY   ROOF

D	O	O	R	S	R	T
A	P	O	I	S	O	N
I	E	R	V	S	O	A
T	N	R	Y	A	F	P

___ ___ ___ ___ ___ ___   ___ ___   ___ ___ ___ ___ ___

If you think you should follow Poison Ivy into the stairwell, go to Chapter 26.

If you want to bring Mr. Freeze to justice, go to Chapter 17.

50

The Joker is not getting away this time, you think, stepping back, lowering your shoulder, and slamming into the door.

The door pops open, but before you can see what or who is inside, a huge explosion goes off.

KA-THOOM!

The door was rigged with explosives set to go off as soon as it was opened.

THE END

51

You dash into the alley, determined not to lose track of Catwoman. You've pursued her for too long to give up the chase now. The alley is dark and dank. The stench of rotting garbage assaults your nostrils. Rats scurry past your feet. You scan the darkness, looking for a clue, hoping for a sign.

There is no movement, no sound. Catwoman, it would appear, has simply vanished into the night. As you turn around to leave, you feel a sharp blow to the back of your head.

Everything goes dark.

THE END

52

You reach for your Utility Belt and grab the self-contained breathing mask you had prepared. But Poison Ivy is too fast. Before you can cover your nose and mouth, she sprays you with her floral toxins.

You drop the mask to the ground as dizziness washes over you. You fight to stay focused but your mind becomes a jumbled haze of confusion. You sink to one knee, then drop flat onto your face. You drift off into unconsciousness, all memory of Poison Ivy's terrorist attack wiped from your mind.

THE END

53

You can't stand it any longer. Anger overwhelms reason. You know this was all too easy. You know the Riddler led you to this spot, and all your training screams out that this is a trap.

But you've been so frustrated trying to stop all these escaped criminals. You're tired of being led around in the dark. He's here, right now, and you're not going to let him get away.

You rush right at the Riddler, readying your body to tackle him, take him down, tie him up, and finally get some answers.

But as you reach the Riddler you pass right through his body, realizing as you do that he is nothing more than a holographic projection. In the split second it takes for your brain to process this, your mind comes to the swift conclusion that this was a trap after all.

THOOM!

By interrupting the holographic beam, you trigger an explosion that brings the warehouse down all around you.

THE END

54

"Let's run a check of Arkham's electrical system, Doctor," you suggest.

"Of course, Batman," Dr. Arkham replies. "I'll set it up now."

You stare impatiently over Dr. Arkham's shoulder at his computer screen, hoping that this test will finally be the light at the end of the tunnel.

The computer runs through a diagnostic program of the electrical system, showing every event that took place in the building during the last month, minute by minute. Most of them are routine—lights switched on and off, electronic doors sliding open and closed, office machines turned on and off.

Then you notice an odd event.

"Look at that, Doctor," you say, leaning forward and pointing at the screen. "It seems that during the power outage, someone managed to open the electronically controlled doors to a handful of cells. Four cells, to be exact."

Dr. Arkham cross-references the cell ID numbers and discovers exactly which cells were opened.

"The cells that were opened were the ones holding Catwoman, Poison Ivy, Mr. Freeze, and the Riddler!" you exclaim.

"But I don't understand," Dr. Arkham says. "Why would someone open the cells but leave the criminals inside?"

"They didn't," you explain. "Look at this. Seconds after those cell doors were opened, a new piece of equipment was installed in each of the four cells. I think if we go back to the cells and check them out, we'll have our answer."

You and Dr. Arkham race to the cell block. At Catwoman's cell you see what appears to be Catwoman sitting inside, smiling at you as she has done the last few times you came to this cell.

"Go ahead and open it, Doctor," you suggest.

"But Batman, Catwoman is right there!" Dr. Arkham protests.

"Actually, she isn't," you reply cryptically. "Trust me."

"Of course, Batman."

Dr. Arkham uses his electronically coded key to open Catwoman's cell. You step into the cell but Catwoman does not acknowledge or even seem to notice your presence. Stepping up onto a chair, you rip open a plastic light fixture and reveal a tiny, but sophisticated-looking piece of equipment hidden there.

"What is that, Batman?" Dr. Arkham asks.

"It's the answer we've been looking for," you reply. Then you grab the device and rip it from the ceiling. Catwoman instantly vanishes.

"It's an intricate holographic projector," you explain. "Obviously, whoever is behind this plot managed to open the cells during the power outage, free the four criminals, and replace them with these projectors—making it appear that they were still safely in their cells. Let's check the others."

One by one you go to cells of the Riddler, Mr. Freeze, and Poison Ivy. In each cell you find the same holo-projector. You remove each one, and the images of the super-villains vanish.

"This is the most detailed and realistic holographic projection system I've ever encountered," you point out. "But now, of course, we know that the criminals are out, on the loose."

If you think you should go back to the Batcave to research the holographic projector system, go to Chapter 32.

If you think you should go after the super-villains, go to Chapter 47.

55

The Joker is the most difficult of all your adversaries to track down. By the time you even get your first lead, the others could have gotten away with many more crimes. So you decide to return to the penthouse art gallery and try to stop Catwoman and the Riddler.

This time, you fly back to the building in the Bat-Copter. You swoop down toward the roof in your one-man flying machine, zooming past the hovering helicopter that is still being loaded with stolen artwork.

But it appears you are just in time.

Catwoman and the Riddler are racing across the roof toward a rope ladder dangling from the open door of the chopper.

"Riddler! I'm here to bring you back to Arkham!" you shout.

"It's not me you want, Batman!" the Riddler yells back. "I'll tell you who is behind all this!"

What kind of trick is this? you wonder as you maneuver the Bat-Copter right next to the getaway chopper.

What else? A riddle! Just before he disappears into the helicopter, the Riddler shouts out a riddle to you.

133

HIDDEN MESSAGE

Find the hidden message in the following sentence.
The Riddler asks: What did the carpenter's tool list say?
Chisel away what's not needed to carve out the answer:

DRILL K. OK. JUST CLEAN IT.
LATHE J. OK. ERASE WOODWORK.
SANDER P. BROKEN. FIX IT!

If you think you should follow the Riddler, go to Chapter 11.

If you think you should pursue the Joker, go to Chapter 41.

56

Deciding that it's more important to stop whoever is behind this whole plot than it is to simply catch Catwoman and the Riddler, you hurry  back down the side of the building, jump into the Batmobile, and speed away.

After a brief stop to change, you speed to the Wayne Enterprises building and take the express elevator to the office of Lucius Fox.

"What have you got, Lucius?" you ask.

"I've been digging into this company, trying to make an educated decision about whether or not we should invest in this new technology," Lucius explains. "I mean, if this holographic system works as well as they say, this really could revolutionize the video game business.

"But the more I dig, the more everything to do with this company points to the same place—a mysterious man with seemingly no identity."

"I suspect that the whole video game company is just a front, Lucius," you explain. "It's just a way to hide the development of this potentially dangerous holo-projector by pretending to create a new video game technology.

"And now you tell me that you seem to have tracked down the man behind all this and that he seems to have no identity. Well, there is only one criminal I can think of who has the resources to pull this off and who has an identity that is totally hidden—the Joker!"

If you think you should try to find the Joker, go to Chapter 41.

If you think you should go after Catwoman and the Riddler, go to Chapter 55.

57

Pivoting on your heel, you turn and fire a grapnel line at a tree branch overhanging the fence surrounding the water park. The line wraps around the branch. Pulling it taut, you leap up and swing out of the park, with Freeze firing blasts all around you.

This is bigger than just Freeze, you think as you speed away in the Batmobile. *I've got to look at this picture from all angles.*

Back in the Batcave, you review all the clues you have gathered so far. You run through all that has happened, going over and over in your mind the strange events of the past few days. And there is only one conclusion you can come to.

The time has come to go to Arkham and find out how all these super-villains you put there have managed to escape.

If you find your four enemies at the end of this maze, go to Chapter 16.

If you reach Arkham Asylum safely, go to Chapter 28.

58

You hurry back to the Batcave to try to make sense of all this. All these criminals who are supposed to be in Arkham are out and committing blatant crimes.

It seems they're all out challenging me. By pulling off these outrageous crimes, they are flaunting the fact that somehow they escaped from Arkham after I put them there. I think the time has come to check in with Dr. Arkham and see—

Suddenly the Batcomputer starts beeping wildly. You rush to the screen and see a flashing message. It's from the Riddler!

Somehow, another of your enemies, the Riddler, has hacked into the Batcave's main computer. Before you can start to do a full system check, the flashing message icon on the screen morphs into a riddle.

You read the riddle, hoping to find some clue. It reads:

"I'm in the ocean but I am dry; sick people see me before they die. What am I?"

If you think the answer to the riddle is "a dock," go to Chapter 21.

If you think the answer to the riddle is "a doc[tor]," go to Chapter 34.

59

You charge right at the Joker. You've found him, the man behind the Arkham escape, the man behind the wild goose chase, the man behind this whole ordeal. You are not going to let him get away. There'll be plenty of time to go after the others once the leader is in your grasp.

The Joker doesn't move. He makes no attempt to get away or elude you. When you go to grab him, you get a big surprise— something that appears to also be a surprise for the other super- villains.

To learn what that surprise is, solve the puzzle.

UNSCRAMBLE

Unscramble the following words and write them in the spaces. Then read down the circled column to learn the Joker's surprise.

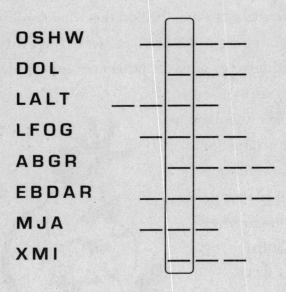

OSHW ＿＿＿＿

DOL ＿＿＿

LALT ＿＿＿＿

LFOG ＿＿＿＿

ABGR ＿＿＿＿

EBDAR ＿＿＿＿＿

MJA ＿＿＿

XMI ＿＿＿

Go to Chapter 23.

Answers

3

27

GO TO ARKHAM

C	G	O	T	O	A
R	I	D	D	L	E
I	R	K	H	A	M
M	I	T	C	I	V
E	S	C	A	P	E

28

ALL THREE ATTACKS ARE REAL

10

two FREE ZEbras HASsle CLUEless
lions   (FREEZE HAS CLUE)

31

19

FROZEN WATER IN SUMMER

24

FREEZE
defend, front, wet, water, zip, breath

25

A NEW PIECE OF EQUIPMENT

A	N	J	E	W	P
T	R	A	P	I	E
C	E	I	O	F	E
C	E	L	L	Q	U
I	P	D	O	O	R
B	L	O	C	K	M
E	N	T	K	E	Y

39

ALLEY TRAP

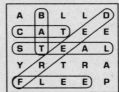

A	B	L	L	D
C	A	T	E	E
S	T	E	A	L
Y	R	T	R	A
F	L	E	E	P

40

TOXIN

start, open, excite, find, night

41

SEWER

chase, send, swim, here, heart

42

ANSWER AT ARKHAM

43

DANGER LURKS BEHIND
THE DOOR

44

45

mend stitch SEW ERase pattern
(SEWER)

46

cha-CHA SEarch for FREE ZEbra
(CHASE FREEZE)

49

STAIRS A TRAP

D	O	O	R	S	R	T
A	P	O	I	S	O	N
I	E	R	V	S	O	A
T	N	R	Y	A	F	P

55

laTHE J. OK. ERase woodwork
(THE JOKER)

57

59

HOLOGRAM

show, old, tall, golf, grab, bread,
jam, mix

Congratulations! You've captured the
super-villains by following this path:
1–39–12–30–20–40–14–9–58–34–
27–38–28–15–24–10–33–42–48–25–
54–32–56–41–6–18–43–37–59–23

OKANAGAN REGIONAL LIBRARY
3 3132 03327 6876